W9-CPE-179

Chicago ABC

A Larry Gets Lost book

Written and Illustrated by
John Skewes

little bigfoot
an imprint of sasquatch books
seattle, wa

Copyright © 2016 by John Skewes

All rights reserved. No portion of this book may be reproduced or utilized in any form, or by any electronic, mechanical, or other means, without the prior written permission of the publisher.

Manufactured in China by C&C Offset Printing Co. Ltd. Shenzhen, Guangdong Province, in November 2015

Published by Little Bigfoot, an imprint of Sasquatch Books
20 19 18 17 16   9 8 7 6 5 4 3 2 1

Editor: Susan Roxborough
Production editor: Em Gale
Design: Mint Design
Interior composition: Joyce Hwang

Library of Congress Cataloging-in-Publication Data is available.

ISBN: 978-1-57061-993-9

Sasquatch Books
1904 Third Avenue, Suite 710
Seattle, WA 98101
(206) 467-4300
www.sasquatchbooks.com
custserv@sasquatchbooks.com

This is **L**arry.

ABCDEFGHIJKLMNOPQRSTUVWXYZ

And this is **P**ete.

Help them find **letters**
as they go down the street . . .

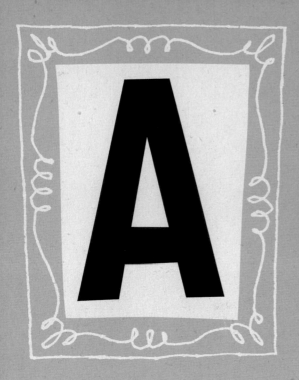

A

is for
Art Institute.

Aa

Shedd Aquarium

And
aquarium.

Bb

B is for **Bulls.** And **Bears.**

Cc

C is for **Cubs.**

D

is for **deep-dish pizza.**

Dd

E

Ee

is for
engineer.

Ff

F is for **Field Museum.**

The Field Museum of Natural History

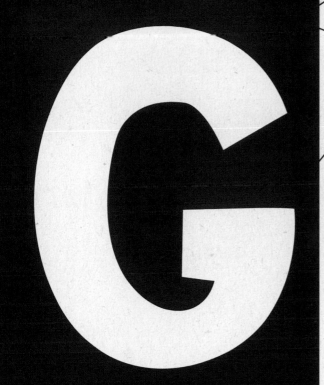

G

is for
Grant Park.

Hh

H

is for
**Hancock
Center.**

John Hancock Center

I is for **ice-skating.**

Jj

J is for jazz.

Kk

K is for kids!

Cloud Gate (The Bean)

Ll

is for
the Loop.

M is for **Magnificent Mile.**

Mm

N is for
Navy Pier.

Nn

Oo

is for
**O'Hare
International
Airport.**

P
is for
Picasso.

Pp

Qq

Q

is for
quick!

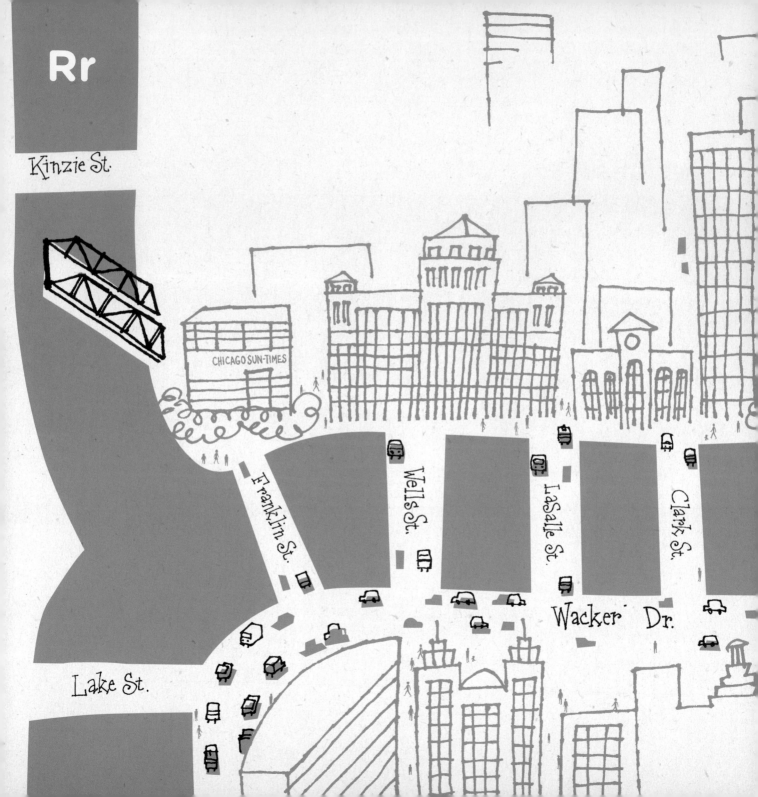

Rr

Kinzie St.

CHICAGO SUN-TIMES

Franklin St.

Wells St.

LaSalle St.

Clark St.

Wacker Dr.

Lake St.

Dearborn St.

STATE St.

Wabash Ave.

Michigan Ave.

R

is for
**Chicago
River.**

Ss

US Cellular Field

is for
White Sox.

T

Tt

is for

taxis.

CHICAGO WATERTAXI

Uu

U

is for
umbrella.

Vv

METRA

V is for **Van Buren.**

Van Buren Street Station

W

is for
Willis
Tower.

Nebraska

IO

KANSAS

M

Ww

Wisconsin

LAKE
Michigan

Michig

NA

X

marks
the spot
where
Chicago is!

souri

Illinois

Indiana

Xx

and **Z** is for **zoo.**

Lincoln Park Zoo

Zz

A B C D E
F G H I J K L
M N O P Q
R S T U V W
X Y Z

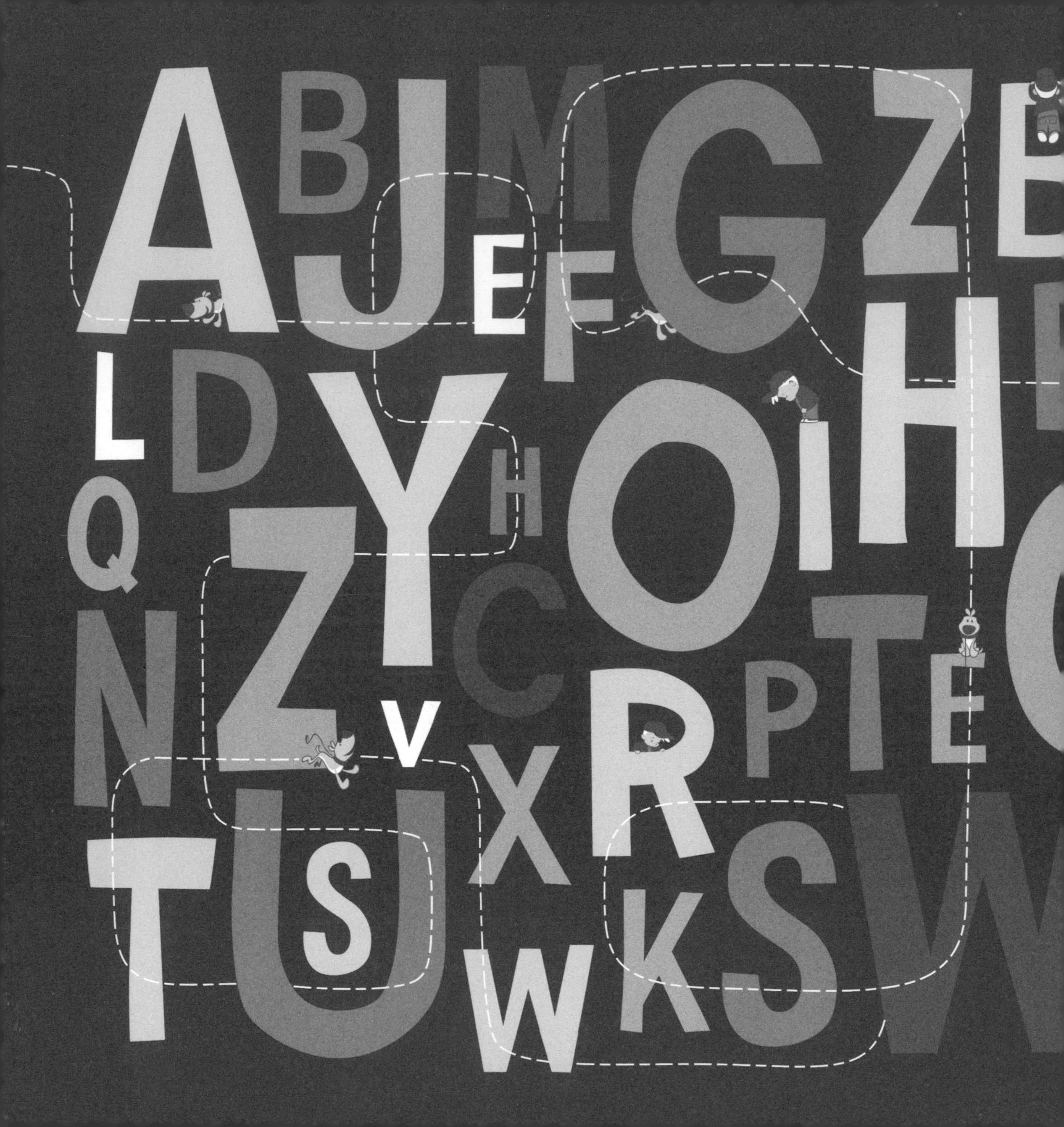